# SHANGHAI SUKKAH

For my brother-in-law, Bruce
Green, a true Tzaddik
—H.S.H.

For my mom and dad who
have made everything possible
—j.j.t.

Text copyright © 2015 by Heidi Smith Hyde
Illustrations copyright © 2015 by Jing Jing Tsong

KAR-BEN PUBLISHING
A division of Lerner Publishing Group, Inc.
241 First Avenue North
Minneapolis, MN 55401 USA
1-800-4-KARBEN

Website address: www.karben.com

Main body text set in Century Gothic Standard 14/19.
Typeface provided by Monotype Typography.

Library of Congress Cataloging-in-Publication Data

Hyde, Heidi Smith.
  Shanghai sukkah / by Heidi Smith Hyde ; illustrated by Jing Jing Tsong.
    pages  cm
  Summary: To escape the Nazis, a young Jewish boy named Marcus and his
family move to Shanghai, where Marcus and his new friend Liang build a sukkah
on the roof and together they celebrate Sukkot and the Chinese Moon Festival.
    ISBN: 978-1-4677-3474-5 (lib. bdg. : alk. paper)
    [1. Sukkah—Fiction.  2. Sukkot—Fiction.  3. Mid-autumn Festival—Fiction.
4. Friendship—Fiction.  5. Refugees—Fiction.  6. Emigration and immigration—
Fiction.  7. Jews—China—Shanghai—Fiction.  8. Shanghai (China)—History—20th
century—Fiction.  9. China—History—1937-1945—Fiction.]  I. Tsong, Jing Jing,
illustrator.  II. Title.
PZ7.H9677Sh 2015
[E]—dc23
                                                                        2014028812

Manufactured in the United States of America
1 – CG – 7/15/15

# Shanghai Sukkah

Heidi Smith Hyde

illustrations by
Jing Jing Tsong

## ON HIS TENTH BIRTHDAY,

Marcus found himself on an ocean liner, headed for Shanghai.

"I don't want to go to China," he whispered to his parents. "I want to stay in Berlin."

But Berlin wasn't safe for Jews anymore. "We need to go where we are welcome, Marcus," Mama said. "I know it won't be easy, but as long as we're together we'll manage somehow. And there are other Jews in Shanghai."

# SHANGHAI WAS NOTHING LIKE BERLIN.

In Berlin, the pavement did not melt during the hot summer months, nor did the streets flood. In Berlin, seven families did not share one room in an old apartment building.

But Mama said to make the best of it, so they did. Every night she put flowers on the table. On Shabbat they lit candles and recited the blessings.

At the yeshiva in downtown Shanghai, Marcus met other Jewish boys his age. One weekend, Marcus and his friends were playing marbles in one of their neighborhood's narrow alleys. Marcus's marble rolled too far. He chased after it, but someone else reached it first.

A Chinese boy held the marble out to Marcus.

"Thank you," said Marcus. He pointed to himself. "I'm Marcus."

The boy smiled shyly. "Liang."

Marcus waved toward his friends. "Want to play with us?"

Liang's smile grew, and he nodded.

Although they spoke different languages, Marcus and Liang soon learned to communicate as only friends do.

Yet Marcus missed his family and friends back home. As the harvest holiday of Sukkot drew near, he felt this loss even more. He thought of the beautiful sukkah his family always made, with fresh fruits and vegetables woven into the branches.

"Where will we build our sukkah this year?" he asked his parents. "The apartment building has no yard or garden."

"Can we use the roof? Nobody uses the roof," Marcus said. He was determined to perform the mitzvah of eating all his meals in the sukkah. "My friends can help me make it. We'll build it out of bamboo."

Two days before Sukkot, Marcus, Liang, and the boys from yeshiva gathered bamboo for the sukkah. Using a saw Liang had borrowed from his father, they cut the stalks and loaded them onto a rickshaw.

Then they collected shrubs and greenery for the s'chach, the roof of the sukkah. As they worked, Marcus told Liang about Sukkot.

"We have a harvest holiday, too," said Liang. "It's called the Moon Festival. There are games and moon-shaped cookies and a lantern parade. We make red lanterns with special riddles attached."

"What kinds of riddles?" asked Marcus.

Liang smiled secretively. "You will find out soon. The Moon Festival begins tomorrow!"

The next day, Marcus and his friends built their rooftop sukkah. Together they measured and cut and fastened. All the while, they sang songs from their old home to pass the time.

It was a simple little sukkah with its slender bamboo poles and sparse roof. Here in Shanghai where supplies were scarce, fruits and vegetables were for eating, not for decorating.

"My sukkah is so plain. I wish it were a little nicer," Marcus told Liang.

"I know how to make you feel better," said Liang. "Come to the Moon Festival tonight with my family and me. We can march in the parade together."

When darkness fell, Marcus followed Liang's family deep into the city, where people of all ages were gathering. The streets of Shanghai exploded with wonder. Bright lights filled the night sky.

"Look—a dragon!" exclaimed Marcus, pointing to a paper creature that stretched from one side of the street to the other.

"Dragons bring good luck," explained Liang.

Then Marcus noticed what looked like a bunch of bright stars twinkling in the distance. The parade of lanterns had begun!

Liang led Marcus to a table covered with shiny, red paper lanterns. Each lantern had a slip of paper attached to it.

"The papers have riddles on them," Liang told Marcus, picking up a lantern. "Let's see what this one says."

He squinted at the words on the paper, then translated for Marcus.

**"What adds light and warmth, even though you can't see it?"**

Marcus thought and thought, but no answers came. What could possibly add light and yet not be seen?

"Come on," said Liang. "Let's join the parade!" The two friends raced down the street, into the sea of lights.

At yeshiva the next morning, Marcus couldn't stop thinking about the riddle of the lantern.

"Rabbi, what adds light and warmth, even though you can't see it?" he asked Rabbi Kravitz.

Stroking his beard thoughtfully, Rabbi Kravitz said, "Your question is a puzzling one, Marcus. How did it come to you?"

"It came from a lantern that my friend gave me," Marcus replied.

Rabbi Kravitz smiled mysteriously. "Perhaps the lantern will light the way to the answer."

At sundown, Mama said, "It's time to recite the blessings, Marcus. Shall we go upstairs to the roof?  Papa and I would like to see the sukkah you and your friends worked so hard to build."

"All right, Mama. But it's not as nice as our sukkah in Berlin," Marcus warned her.

But up on the roof, Marcus's breath caught in his throat. There, glittering in the darkness, stood the little bamboo sukkah, covered in red paper lanterns of all shapes and sizes.

"Happy Sukkot," cried Liang with a smile as bright as the full moon.

Marcus gazed at the beautifully decorated sukkah. It was the best sukkah ever, but not just because of the lanterns. What made it special, thought Marcus, was the friend who decorated it.

Marcus thought again about the riddle of the lantern.

**"What adds light and warmth, even though you can't see it?"**

**The answer, Marcus decided, was friendship.**

# Historical note

In the 1930s, before World War II began, many European Jews felt that to ensure their safety they needed to leave their homes, but they had nowhere to go. Most nations would not accept large numbers of emigrating Jews. But one country's doors opened wide. Between 1938 and 1941, thousands of Jewish refugees escaped by steamship to China. Chiune Sugihara, a Japanese diplomat, issued thousands of visas to Jews at the risk of his own career. Those visas permitted Jewish refugees to travel first to Japan and then to Shanghai.

The Jews settled in Hongkew, the poorest section of Shanghai, which came to be called the Shanghai Ghetto. Several families might share a single tiny, rented room without lighting or indoor plumbing. The refugees endured disease and too little food.

**The Hongkew district in Shanghai became home to thousands of European Jews during World War II.**

**Jewish refugees in Shanghai lived in crowded buildings like this one.**

Despite the difficult conditions, Jewish culture flourished. Along the narrow, winding streets, it wasn't unusual to find Yiddish theater, coffee houses, synagogues, and schools. Newspapers and libraries were established, and Jewish holidays and kashrut were observed. There was even a yeshiva, known as the Mirrer Yeshiva.

Thanks to the efforts of the American Jewish Joint Distribution Committee, soup kitchens and makeshift hospitals were also founded to assist Jewish refugees who arrived on China's shores.

During a time when most countries looked the other way, China offered a haven, saving the lives of thousands of Jews from Lithuania, Poland, Austria, Russia, and Germany.

**Jewish refugees lived alongside Chinese residents of Shanghai.**

**Many Jews lived in these buildings on Word Street in Shanghai, shown in this 1939 photograph.**

Images are used with the permission of: Beatrice Reubens, Yad Vashem (Hongkew district, group photo); courtesy of Beit Hatfutsot – The Museum of the Jewish People (home interior, balcony); photo by H.P. Witting, courtesy of Fred Dranich, Yad Vashem (group of men).

**Jewish residents of Shanghai, like these Hasidic Jewish men standing under a Chinese street sign, brought their traditions with them to China.**